Grade 3 Clarinet

grade 3 clarinet pieces

CW00494603

Chester Music
part of The Music Sales Group

London/New York/Paris/Sydney/Copenhagen/Berlin/Madrid/Hong Kong/Tokyo

Published by

Chester Music
part of The Music Sales Group
14-15 Berners Street, London W1T 3LJ, UK.

Exclusive Distributors:
Music Sales Limited
Distribution Centre, Newmarket Road,
Bury St Edmunds, Suffolk IP33 3YB, UK.

Music Sales Pty Limited
Level 4, Lisgar House,
30-32 Carrington Street,
Sydney, NSW 2000 Australia.

Order No. CH84095
ISBN 978-1-78558-067-3
This book © Copyright 2015 Chester Music Limited.
All Rights Reserved.

Edited by Jenni Norey.
Arranged and engraved by Christopher Hussey.
With thanks to Sandra Gamba.

Printed in the EU.

Clarinet Fingering Chart

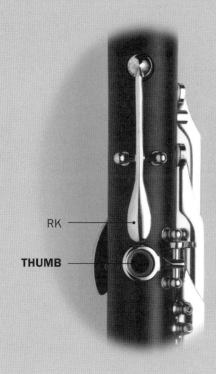

RK

THUMB

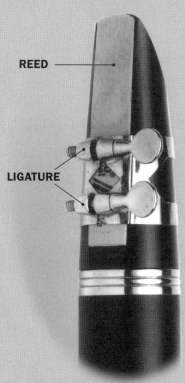

REED

LIGATURE

Mouthpiece

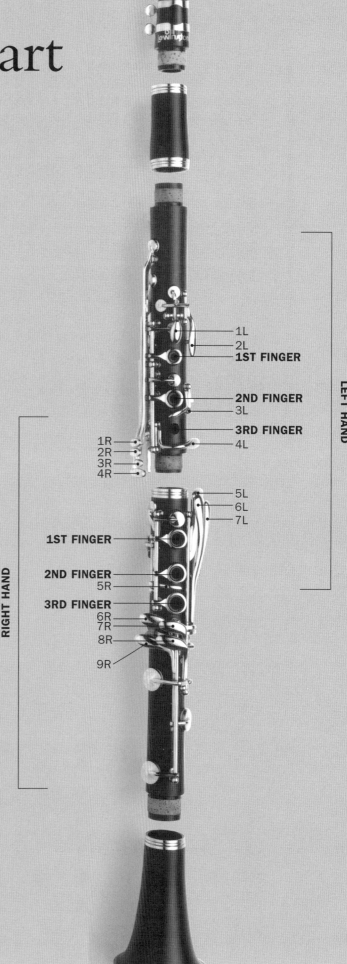

1L
2L
1ST FINGER

2ND FINGER
3L

3RD FINGER
4L

1R
2R
3R
4R

5L
6L
7L

1ST FINGER

2ND FINGER
5R

3RD FINGER
6R
7R
8R
9R

LEFT HAND

RIGHT HAND

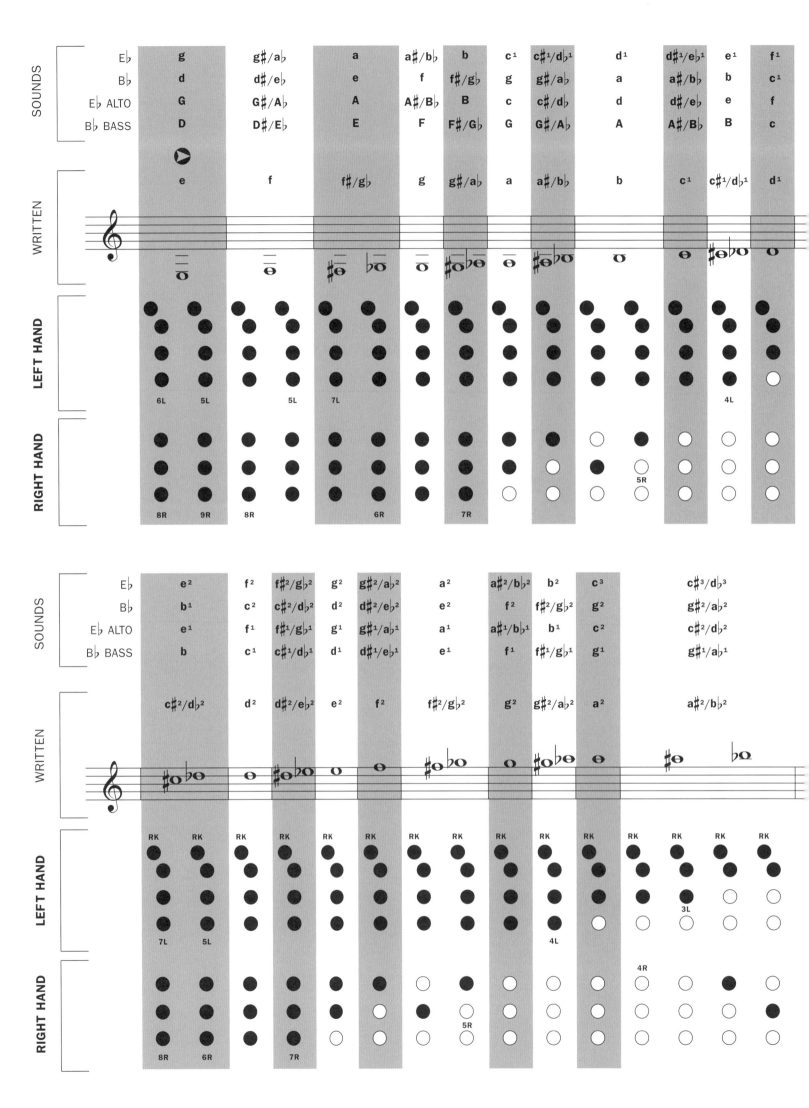

Indicates the lower limit of the best playing range for E♭, B♭, E♭ Alto and B♭ Bass Clarinets

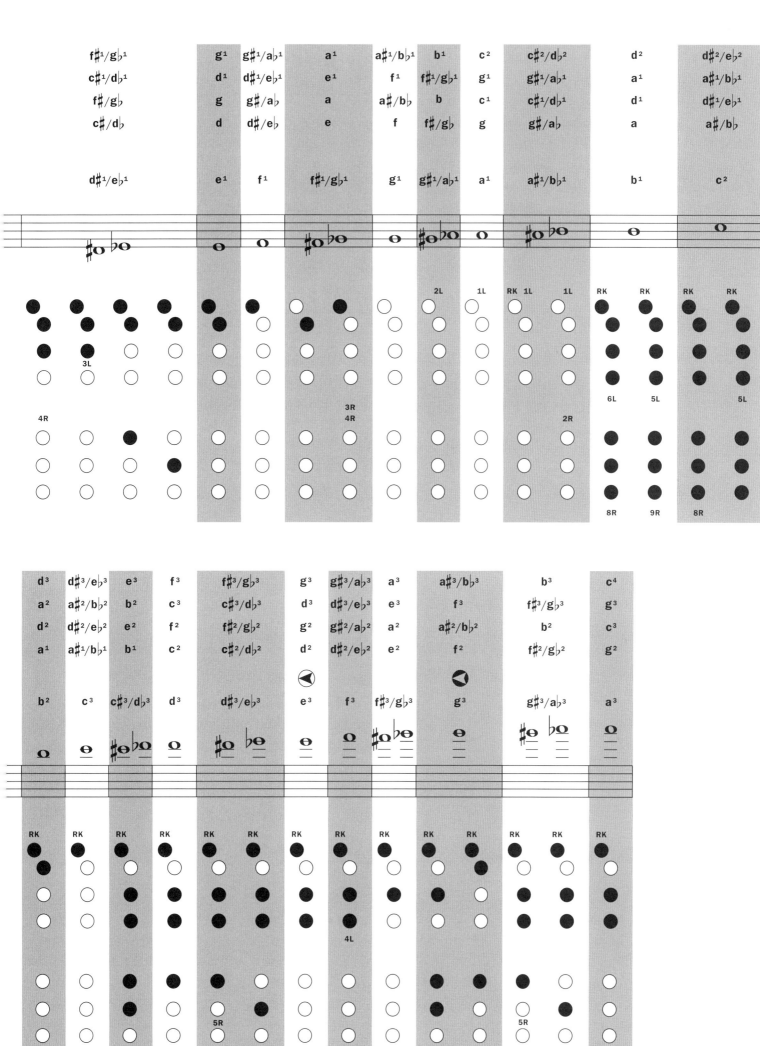

Indicates the upper limit of the best playing range for E♭ and B♭ Clarinets   Indicates the upper limit of the best playing range for E♭ Alto and B♭ Bass Clarinets

All Of Me
John Legend

This simple but effective piano and vocal based song hit the No. 1 spot in several countries, including the US, Australia, Ireland and Canada. It was written for John Legend's then-fiancé Chrissy Teigen, who he married in 2013. The video shows clips from the couple's honeymoon.

Dancing Queen
ABBA

The ultimate disco song that finally made ABBA big in the United States was originally called 'Boogaloo'. It was No. 1 Stateside and almost everywhere else in 1976. The drum part was inspired by George McCrae's 1974 disco hit 'Rock Your Baby'.

Downtown
Petula Clark

British singer Petula Clark is best known for her upbeat popular international hits of the 1960s. Released in four different languages in late 1964, 'Downtown' was a huge success in the UK, France (in both English and French versions), Netherlands, Germany, Australia, Italy, and even Rhodesia and India.

The First Cut Is The Deepest
Cat Stevens

Written by Cat Stevens in 1965, the first person to release this song was P.P. Arnold in May 1967. Steven's own version appeared on his second album *New Masters* later the same year, and the song went on to be covered by many different artists, most notably Rod Stewart and Sheryl Crow.

Hey Jude
The Beatles

Paul was inspired to pen this lyric to console John Lennon's son, Julian, but eventually decided to change the name. At the time it was the longest 45rpm single ever released, clocking in at seven minutes 11 seconds!

Jar Of Hearts
Christina Perri

This bittersweet song about a serial heartbreaker that Christina Perri once dated became a hit in the US after it was featured on the TV show *So You Think You Can Dance?* and then on *Glee*. It spent 22 weeks in the UK charts, peaking at No. 4, and in November 2011 she performed it on the BBC's *Strictly Come Dancing* results show.

Just The Way You Are
Bruno Mars

Launching Bruno Mars into the pop stratosphere, 'Just the Way You Are' was the soulful singer-songwriter's debut single, released to worldwide acclaim in 2010. Inspired by Joe Cocker's 'You Are So Beautiful' and 'Wonderful Tonight' by Eric Clapton, the track is among the best-selling singles of all time, having sold 12.5 million copies.

Let It Be
The Beatles

The last Beatles single to be released, 'Let It Be' was issued on 6 March 1970. It is one of a few Beatles songs that exist in more than one authorised version. It was thought to be a plea for the Beatles to make their peace with each other as they started their solo careers.

Panic Cord
Gabrielle Aplin

British singer-songwriter Gabrielle Aplin first entered the charts with her piano-led cover of Frankie Goes To Hollywood's 'The Power Of Love', which was featured in the 2012 John Lewis Christmas TV advert. 'Panic Cord' is taken from her top 10 debut album *English Rain*.

Right Place Right Time
Olly Murs

'Right Place Right Time' is the title track to Olly Murs' third album. Featuring breakbeats and a prodding, rhythmic piano line that may be more familiar with electronic dance listeners, the song once again breathed fresh ideas into Murs' sound. Bursting with euphoric energy, the track was chosen as the penultimate song for the *Right Place Right Time* tour set list.

Roar
Katy Perry

As the lead single from Katy Perry's fourth studio album, *Prism*, 'Roar' was a huge international hit for the star, topping the charts in 14 countries including the UK, Australia, Canada, Ireland and New Zealand. Based on the idea of self-empowerment and standing up for yourself, the song's video features Perry playing the role of a plane crash survivor in the jungle who learns to conquer her environment by finding her inner tiger.

Skyfall
from *Skyfall*

Skyfall is the third Bond film to star Daniel Craig and the 23rd in the 007 franchise. It is one of only six films to feature the iconic Aston Martin DB5. Sung by Adele, who co-wrote the theme with Paul Epworth, this song is a strong power ballad comparable to the old Bond themes sung by Shirley Bassey.

Someone Like You
Adele

Adele's breathtaking performance of this song at the 2011 BRIT Awards led to it becoming her first No. 1 single in the UK, a position it held for five weeks. It tells the story of Adele learning of her ex-boyfriend's engagement and wishing him happiness whilst still longing to find 'someone like him'.

Thinking Out Loud
Ed Sheeran

Ed Sheeran famously wrote 'Thinking Out Loud' using a guitar gifted to him by Harry Styles of One Direction, yet piano features heavily on this steady-paced ballad that celebrates the enduring quality of love and romance.

Titanium
David Guetta

Despite being offered to several vocalists, including Katy Perry, David Guetta's 'Titanium' was finally released with the artist who co-wrote the song and recorded the demo singing lead vocals: Australian singer Sia. This song proved a big hit for both of them, claiming a top 10 spot in over 15 countries.

All Of Me

Words & Music by John Stephens and Toby Gad

Play a B♭ major scale to prepare for this song. Take away the ties and slurs in bars 22–25 at first, in order to secure the rhythm, and use legato tonguing throughout.

Dancing Queen

Words & Music by Benny Andersson, Stig Anderson & Björn Ulvaeus

Play a D major scale to prepare. Remember to count two minim beats per bar. Try lifting off after the dotted crotchets a little earlier so there is a slight separation—this will give the music bounce and energy.

Downtown

Words & Music by Tony Hatch

Watch out for the crotchet triplets in bar 17—they are played over two crotchet beats. Practise bars 18–21 without the ties and slurs until the rhythm is secure.

Make sure you perform the dynamics as written.

The First Cut Is The Deepest

Words & Music by Cat Stevens

Play a D major scale to prepare. *Cantabile* tells you to play in a 'singing style'—don't force the tone, and keep your airstream steady.

Be careful of your tone in bar 20–21—smiling and making an 'ee' mouth shape will help.

Hey Jude

Words & Music by John Lennon & Paul McCartney

Practise the rhythm in bars 11 and 16 on its own, and without slurs and ties until you are confident.

Make a contrast between the *forte* dynamic (marked *f*) in bars 20–22 and the *mezzo piano* (*mp*) when you repeat from the sign (𝄋).

Jar Of Hearts

Words & Music by Christina Perri, Drew Lawrence & Barrett Yeretsian

Use legato tonguing throughout and make sure the tongued semiquavers are clean.

Just The Way You Are

Words & Music by Ari Levine, Bruno Mars, Philip Lawrence, Khari Cain & Khalil Walton

Perfect the rhythm in bars 9–12 before moving on. Make sure you really lift the staccato quaver Ds—use a light tonguing action with lots of air support.

Be careful of your tone from bar 24 to the end—smiling and making an 'ee' mouth shape will help.

Let It Be

Words & Music by John Lennon & Paul McCartney

Play a D major scale to prepare, and make sure you know the fingering for low F♯. Remember to count two minim beats per bar, and use legato tonguing throughout.

Panic Cord

Words & Music by Jez Ashurst, Gabrielle Aplin & Nicholas Atkinson

Be sure to tongue the second semiquaver in bars 14 and 15—this articulation also occurs in a number of other places. Remember the B♭s throughout.

Right Place Right Time

Words & Music by Stephen Robson, Claude Kelly & Oliver Murs

Make sure you execute the correct articulation. Watch your tone from the Ds to the high Bs in the chorus (for example, in bars 24 and 28).

Roar

Words & Music by Max Martin, Lukasz Gottwald, Bonnie McKee, Katy Perry & Henry Russell Walter

From bar 18 to the second note of bar 22, leave your right-hand fingers down (including the Gs and As). The same applies for bars 23–26 and bars 27–30. In bar 28 and 29, the staccato and slur over the C means to 'throw the note away' so it is light, but not tongued.

Skyfall

Words & Music by Paul Epworth & Adele Adkins

Listen out for your tone when playing the 'throat notes' (Gs, As and B♭s) as they are quite weak—put down some right-hand fingers to help the tuning and sound.

dim. al niente tells you to diminuendo to nothing.

Someone Like You

Words & Music by Daniel Wilson & Adele Adkins

Be precise with your articulation in bars 17–20, and use legato tonguing throughout. Watch out for the quaver triplets in bar 22, and make sure the semiquavers are even at the end of bar 26.

Leave your right-hand fingers down for the Gs in bar 24 to help make going back up to the C smoother.

Thinking Out Loud

Words & Music by Ed Sheeran & Amy Wadge

Watch out for the quaver triplets in this song. In bars 30, 32 and 34, the quaver rest is part of the triplet, so you could practise adding another C in its place and then omitting it when you are confident.

The high Cs (bars 30–34) can sound quite shrill, especially when played loud. You should make an 'ee' shape with your mouth and smile to help tame them!

Titanium

Words & Music by Sia Furler, David Guetta, Giorgio Tuinfort & Nick van de Wall

Count the ties carefully throughout. Be careful with the sound of your 'throat notes' (As and B♭s).

Make sure the *fortissimo* (**ff**) at the end is really big, but watch your tone—a slightly firm embouchure for the As will help.

123456789

COLLECT THE SERIES
Graded Clarinet Pieces
15 Popular Practice Pieces

Grade 1 Clarinet Pieces
CH84073

Grade 2 Clarinet Pieces
CH84084

Grade 3 Clarinet Pieces
CH84095

Available from all good music shops
or, in case of difficulty contact:
Music Sales Limited, Newmarket Road, Bury St Edmunds, Suffolk, IP33 3YB, UK.
music@musicsales.co.uk

HOW TO DOWNLOAD YOUR MUSIC TRACKS

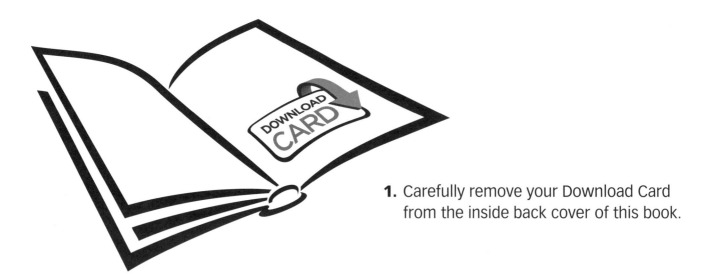

1. Carefully remove your Download Card from the inside back cover of this book.

2. On the back of the card is your unique access code. Enter this at www.musicsalesdownloads.com

TO REDEEM THIS CARD VISIT
www.musicsalesdownloads.com

ENTER ACCESS CODE:

XXXXXXXXX

Download Cards are powered by Dropcards.
User must accept terms at dropcards.com/terms
which are adopted by The Music Sales Group.
Not redeemable for cash. Void where prohibited or restricted by law.

DCARD1006478

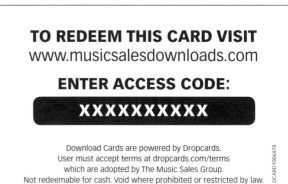

3. Follow the instructions to save your files to your computer*. That's it!